Meet Winslow Whale

Created and illustrated by

JOYCE HOWELL

Story by

B. G. HENNESSY

Viking

The art was prepared with gouache on bristol plate.

VIKING
Published by the Penguin Group
Penguin Books USA Inc., 375 Hudson Street, New York, New York 10014, U.S.A.
Penguin Books Ltd, 27 Wrights Lane, London W8 5TZ, England
Penguin Books Australia Ltd, Ringwood, Victoria, Australia
Penguin Books Canada Ltd, 10 Alcorn Avenue, Toronto, Ontario, Canada M4V 3B2
Penguin Books (N.Z.) Ltd, 182-190 Wairau Road, Auckland 10, New Zealand

Penguin Books Ltd, Registered Offices: Harmondsworth, Middlesex, England

First published in 1994 by Viking, a division of Penguin Books USA Inc.

1 3 5 7 9 10 8 6 4 2

Library of Congress Catalog Card Number: 94-60253
ISBN 0-670-85632-0

Printed in Singapore
Set in Oliver

For my two daughters, Hannah and Damaris

—J.H.

On the day Winslow was born the sun sparkled on the surface of the sea like a million birthday candles.

Winslow's parents were overjoyed to have a baby of their own. They had always been kind to all the sea creatures, and the sea kingdom was especially happy to hear of Winslow's arrival. As soon as Winslow's father announced the news, the dolphins told the sea bass, the sea bass told the guppies, and the guppies told the puffer fish, who puffed up with delight. Within two tides every creature in the seven seas knew that Winslow was born.

There are many strange and remarkable creatures that live in the seas. But right from the beginning it was clear that there was something unusual about Winslow—unusual even for a sea creature. There were three bright red hearts where Winslow's spout should be!

No one in all the oceans had ever seen anything quite like it.

Everyone wondered what the hearts were for, because under the sea there is a reason for everything.

Were they a disguise? A lure for food? Perhaps for protection? It was a mystery.

As Winslow grew he worried more and more about his hearts. "I don't like being different," he told his parents. "I want to be like all the other whales."

"Winslow, we all are different in some way," they said. "It's just that you are a little more different. We don't know what your hearts are for yet. Only you will be able to figure that out, and this will take some time."

His parents' explanation did not make Winslow feel one bit better. He decided to go for a long swim. Maybe the exercise would help him think.

Winslow loved the open ocean. He loved the hugeness of it, the rhythm of the waves and the taste of the salt.

After swimming twenty miles, Winslow felt much better. He drifted right below the surface of the sea—below, that is, except for the three red hearts.

Cradled by the rolling waves, Winslow was not quite asleep and not quite awake when he felt something pull at his hearts.

Frightened, he leaped out of the water. Water and whale were everywhere.

"Jumping jellyfish!" sputtered a wet and angry seagull. "You almost drowned me!"

"What were you doing to my hearts?" cried Winslow.

"I'm sorry, I didn't know they were a part of you. My name is Henrietta. Really, I am sorry about pecking at you, but those hearts looked so pretty floating on top of the water."

"You actually wanted one of my hearts?" Winslow couldn't believe it.

"You mean you don't want them?" Henrietta couldn't believe that.

Then Winslow told her the whole story.

"Amazing," said Henrietta. "Do you realize how lucky you are? You're one of a kind, unique. Maybe if we put our heads together we can figure out what those hearts do. . . ."

Henrietta and Winslow spent the afternoon trying to solve the mystery. Although Winslow still didn't like his hearts, he loved talking to Henrietta.

When the sun began to set, Henrietta had to fly back to land. "I'll miss you, Winslow. But I'll always be able to find you again, because of your hearts. You'll never be able to pick me out of all the millions of gulls," she said sadly. "I wish I had a heart like one of yours."

Then a remarkable thing happened. One of Winslow's hearts began to tingle; then it tickled; then it turned into two little hearts, and one floated right over to Henrietta!

"Henrietta, look! Now we know what my hearts are for. They're a gift for true friends," said Winslow.

"Winslow, I know I'm special now. Not because of the heart, but because I am your friend." Then Henrietta's heart got smaller and smaller—until it was just the right size to fit under her wing. And Winslow's little heart got bigger and bigger—until it was just the right size to go over his spout.

For a long time Winslow watched Henrietta fly away. Then he began to swim home.

When Winslow's parents heard the whole story they were proud of Winslow and how he had solved the mystery.

Winslow was tired from the exercise of his swim and the excitement of finding and being a friend. It had been a big day for a little whale, and it didn't take long for him to fall asleep.

The next morning Winslow woke up rested and ready from the tip of his fluke to the top of his hearts.

"Off so early, Winslow?" asked his mother.

Winslow smiled. "I sure am. I have lots more friends to meet!" And he swam off in the warm morning sun to find them.